Brent Medeiros has always had a dream of becoming an acclaimed author. Fuelled by a lifelong love of storytelling, he has used any spare time he's been able to find to write as a way of expressing himself. Sunrise is Brent's first work he provides a realistic work exploring the love and devotion between two people and how they can overcome anything together. Brent currently resides in Connecticut and when he is not writing he is a teacher, a movie aficionado, and an avid sports fan.

For B. J. M.

Love you forever, my brother. And to everyone who has always supported my dreams. Thank you.

# Brent Medeiros

## SUNRISE

AUSTIN MACAULEY PUBLISHERS™

LONDON • CAMBRIDGE • NEW YORK • SHARJAH

Copyright © Brent Medeiros 2024

The right of Brent Medeiros to be identified as author of this work has been asserted by the author in accordance with sections 77 and 78 of the Copyright, Designs and Patents Act 1988.

All rights reserved. No part of this publication may be reproduced, stored in a retrieval system, or transmitted in any form or by any means, electronic, mechanical, photocopying, recording, or otherwise, without the prior permission of the publishers.

Any person who commits any unauthorised act in relation to this publication may be liable to criminal prosecution and civil claims for damages.

This is a work of fiction. Names, characters, businesses, places, events, locales, and incidents are either the products of the author's imagination or used in a fictitious manner. Any resemblance to actual persons, living or dead, or actual events is purely coincidental.

A CIP catalogue record for this title is available from the British Library.

ISBN 9781035869848 (Paperback)
ISBN 9781035869855 (ePub e-book)

www.austinmacauley.com

First Published 2024
Austin Macauley Publishers Ltd®
1 Canada Square
Canary Wharf
London
E14 5AA

Every sunrise, Peter would awaken to the sweet sound of her voice calling to him like a song from a bird chirping outside of his window. After a warm shower and getting dressed, he would walk downstairs where she was waiting with a smile adorning her face as bright as the now-risen sun. Each day, Peter and Lily created moments that left imprints in their memories forever. Fate brought these two souls together. Wherever they went, their hands would be clasped together palm to palm, fingers intertwined and locked, fitting like pieces to a puzzle. By the time the sky began to paint itself with shades of red and purple, thanks to a lovely sunset, and once those colours gave way to the black canvas of night, Peter and Lily sat at the kitchen table with a meal they cooked together, laughing and loving each other. After all these years, Peter still found her to be the most beautiful woman his eyes ever saw. When the evening called for sleep, that perfect-fitting puzzle was once again put together and hand-in-hand the two soul mates went to bed. Laying in Peter's arms after a goodnight kiss was how Lily would fall asleep. Peter would slide his fingers through white hair that once was a shimmering blonde. He whispered into her ear that she was his beautiful flower. Then he placed his lips to her wrinkled forehead for one more goodnight kiss. Then he thought about how his life with her began before conceding to sleep.

At sunrise, the smell of rotten eggs seemed to fill the air. There were large clouds of smoke, and in the distance, it seemed there were the faint sounds of yelling. As he slowly came to his senses, Peter realised he was lying on his back with the cold mud soaking into his clothing. His bottom lip quivered as he slowly managed to lift his head. That's when he saw it—the blood soaking through his pants. The crimson puddle was so absorbed by his pant leg that the sight of it made him toss his head to try and keep the vomit from spewing forth from his lips. The pain was setting in and he managed to let out a cry for help. Peter was not meant for war but had been chosen to come and fight anyways. In his ears, his screams sounded loud but they were not reverberating as far, he thought. Finally, Peter gave up and tossed his head back, feeling the squishy mud suck in around his skull. He closed his eyes and began to make his peace with his God before he bled to death. That's when he felt a soft hand touch his arm. His brown eyes slowly opened, and kneeling over him was a blue-eyed angel. She was wearing white and speaking in a soft tone that took him a moment to hear.

"You're going to be okay," the soft voice said. Peter tried to force a nod but he was fixated on those blue eyes. He was lost within them, swimming in their depths. He slowly reached out his hand and his angel took it within hers. Peter smiled and the world went black.

Peter must've slept all night. When he awoke, he noticed that the morning sun was rising. His eyes blinked a few times. The room was silent. There were no smells of burning gunpowder or men moaning. He was able to sit up to see he was in a clean shirt and clean pair of pants. Although his leg was bandaged tight, the pain was relatively gone. A sigh of relief was let go from Peter's lungs because he knew he hadn't died. Then a small smile broke out across his face. That's when he heard that familiar voice.

"Well, look at you smiling. This is good." Peter looked up and immediately sank back into those blue eyes. He stared for a few minutes, but in his mind, it was hours before his throat finally cleared.

"You. I've seen you before." His angel smiled at him with a nod of her head shaking blonde curls.

"Well, yes you did. And you were pretty muddy and not in such great shape." Peter pushed himself up straighter in the bed, being careful to not shift his injured leg.

"You saved me."

"No I didn't," she said.

Peter replied, "But I saw you. I felt you hold my hand."

"It's what I do. I'm a nurse and I help tend to the wounded."

"It's a clear sign that you were supposed to find me. I am forever grateful you did."

"I've always loved to help people."

"You are as beautiful as an angel sent from heaven," Peter stunned himself with that last line and couldn't believe it escaped his lips. His cheeks turned a bright red. All she could do was chuckle behind a smile.

"You're very sweet," she said.

"Peter. My name is… I'm Peter."

"It's a pleasure to meet you, Peter. Lilliana, but you can just call me Lily. But for now I have other patients to look in on. You just lie back and rest. We'll have you healed up in no time." Peter nodded his head and lay back down as his lips pulled up into the biggest smile. Lily thought that he had an adorable smile and told him so before she left his room. Peter whispered to himself, "Lily. Like the beautiful flower," before he closed his eyes to get some more rest.

The next morning, just as the sun was beginning to peek through the clouds, Peter watched as Lily came to his bedside once again to check on him and make sure he was eating and taking his medications. He would tell her his leg was feeling much better and they would sit and converse about their families, where they were from and how they both liked reading and going to the movies. Peter told Lily that when he was all healed up and the war was over, he was going to find her and take her to a movie. She always smiled at that and found him endearing. After a few weeks, Peter was no longer just lying in bed. Every early sunrise, Lily would come and check on him only to find him up and about bragging how his leg felt so good and how he didn't need a cane to walk with. Lily found herself liking Peter more and more but they both knew the time would come when he would be sent back with this platoon. They didn't talk about that much but as they grew to know more about each other, they became closer and closer. One morning when Lily came to see how Peter was doing, he was sitting on the edge of the bed dressed in his uniform. His head was down and he was twiddling his fingers. Immediately she walked over to him and sat down on the bed. Her head rested on his shoulder as his hand found hers. Not many words needed to be spoken. They both felt it. They knew what was there between them. After minutes of silence, Peter pressed his lips to the top of her head and whispered, "You and I met for a reason."

"I… I don't want you to go."

"I know," Peter said, "but we can write. I'll send a letter as often as I can. I'm not going to lose you. Ever. Do you remember that when you found me lying out there clinging to life that the sun was just starting to rise?"

Lily nodded her head yes. "Every time we get a letter from each other, we will open it at sunrise. No matter the day or the month, we can always share a sunrise."

Lily looked into Peter's eyes. Blue now sinking into browns as a small tear left the corner of her eye and slowly made its way down the slope of her cheek before its path was cut off by the gentleness of Peter's thumb. He leant in and kissed her. The spark they felt was undeniable. It felt like two hearts beat as one. They didn't break the kiss for several minutes. When it was finally over, he squeezed her hand as he stood up. As soon as he got his next destination, he'd write to her, to which she replied how'd she'll be waiting with baited breath to read his letters and send her own in return. Peter moved from the room and before she rose from the bed, Lily leant over and pressed her face into the pillow to inhale his scent once more. Never did she think she'd fall for someone she helped nurse but what she felt when around Peter were feelings she could not describe. Throughout the rest of the war, Peter and Lily wrote to each other every day and as they promised each other, they would tear open the envelope at sunrise and with eager anticipation let the words written upon the paper soak into their hearts and minds. Peter would share about the towns he'd been to and the people that he met and to Lily's relief, he hadn't seen any more combat. In return, Lily would write about her patients and the joy she got when they healed, knowing she took some small part in that.

When the war finally came to an end, both Peter and Lily returned home. As they migrated back into a regular life, the letters to each other never ceased. During their earlier correspondence, they had shared addresses so they'd be able to always keep in touch. Adjusting back to a regular life felt weird for both of them. Lily never married.

Instead, she focused on her nursing career. Peter never married either. His one true love was living on the pieces of paper he received almost weekly. Peter struggled to place himself back into a regular life. The army and his comrades were all he knew and now once home, he was living alone and his friends were sparse. One wintry evening, Peter was driving himself to the store. The snow was falling down at a steadily rapid pace which made the little dots of white look furious as they blanketed the ground. In the blink of an eye, Peter felt the car starting to veer off to the side of the road. In a panicked reaction, he jerked the steering wheel to the left and then again to the right. His booted foot pressed down on the brake pedal only to feel it lock up. Under his gloves knuckles were as white as the snow from the extremely tight grip he had on the steering wheel. As fast as the car slid, it came to an abrupt stop. Peter didn't hear the bang or really feel much. The front of his car was smashed against a tree. He felt a small warmth trickling down his forehead before his eyes shut and everything went black. Faint voices were heard and a loud noise that sounded like a siren. Then there was black again.

After what felt like minutes, Peter's eyes slowly opened and as they adjusted to the light, he didn't recognise the ceiling. He tried to sit up but there was a sharp pain in his side and his left arm was in a sling.

*What's this in my nose?* he thought and he reached his good arm up to pull at it.

A voice spoke up, "No sir. You need to keep that in." Peter's eyes widened and showed a look of panic. The voice was calm as they spoke a few more words that Peter couldn't really understand because he was falling back asleep. Once again, he awoke and standing over him was a doctor and a nurse.

*That's not my Lily,* he thought.

The doctor cleared his throat and let Peter know that he was very lucky. He cracked a few ribs and has a sprained shoulder. A few days there in the hospital with rest was what was recommended before being discharged home. Peter nodded. He had no one to go home to anyways.

The doctor left the room and the nurse turned to him and asked, "Is there anything else you need?"

Right away, his mind went to Lily and their sunrise letters. "A pen and paper would be nice." The nurse smiled and told him to get some rest and relax. Peter did just that and fell asleep once again. This time when he woke up, there was a pen and paper sitting on the tray in front of him. Before he began to write, he did say a little prayer to the man above that it was his non-writing arm that was hurt. Almost immediately, he began to put pen to paper and write to Lily. Once he got out of here, he'd had a bunch of letters to mail.

*Surely she'd be concerned she hasn't received any letters from me,* he thought.

Peter became engrossed in writing and didn't notice the nurses coming in and out of his room unless they told it was time to take his medication or to place a food tray in front of him, which Peter actually liked. Hospital food was better than eating hardtack and dried meats out in the middle of a cold, damp field. Just as he finished up the last letter, a voice called out to him. Was it time for more medication already? Peter's eyes looked up ready to accept the small paper cup with the pills inside and a cup of water and she was standing there. It was Lily. Peter couldn't believe it. He rubbed his eyes to make sure he wasn't seeing things. She walked over to the bedside and placed her hand on his as she leaned forward and kissed him. No more words needed to be spoken. She was here. As the kiss broke all Peter could do was smile as a small drop of wetness formed in the corner of his eyes then slid down his cheek. Lily's thumb wiped it away as her own happy tears formed.

"What… How… What are you doing here?" Peter asked.

"I didn't get any letters for a few weeks. I got scared and came to see if you were okay."

"Lily," Peter smiled. "I love you. I don't deserve you but I love you."

Lily said nothing for a moment. She stood next to him, tears in her eyes. Her hand slipped into his. "I love you too. But for the love of God, we have to stop seeing each other like this."

"You mean you don't want to keep rushing to my side every time I almost get killed?" Peter smirked with a bit of joking in his voice.

"Not really. I prefer my men alive."

Peter and Lily laughed. He shifted over in the bed and she slid onto it to lie next to him.

For the remaining days in the hospital, Lily would remain by Peter's side.

After a few days, Peter was discharged and sent home with Lily by his side. His ribs were still hurting a little but his shoulder was healing well and he told her it was because he had a wonderful nurse here at home. The time for Lily to go back home was vastly approaching. They were sitting on the couch holding hands. Peter looked into her eyes.

"I don't want you to go."

"I don't want to go"

"Stay with me, Lily. Don't leave."

There was a small silence that followed before Lily placed her head on Peter's shoulder. She could hear his heart beating from underneath his shirt. Her face turned towards his chest and she murmured, "I want to stay with your forever."

"What?" he said.

She lifted her head and looked into his eyes. Her hand touched his cheek. "I want to stay with you forever, Peter."

Peter smiled and kissed her long and deep. When the kiss broke, he couldn't stop smiling.

"Marry me."

"Right now!?" Lily asked in total surprise.

"Now. Tomorrow. Next week. Ten years from now. I don't care. Just say you'll marry me."

"Yes. Peter. Yes!" Lily's face hurt from smiling and her eyes became teary. Peter's hand lifted and his thumb swiped the tears, leaving a little wetness on her cheeks. He leaned forward and his forehead touched hers.

"You make me so damn happy. That day I woke up and you were standing over me taking care of me, I knew then and there that I loved you." Lily smiled and they embraced and kissed once more.

The reception for the wedding wasn't an elaborate one. It was simple yet elegant.

Their guests were treated to a fun evening of good food and a lot of dancing. Peter and Lily had done a small exchanging of vows and sealed their marriage with a kiss in front of a roaring gathering of their families and closest friends. What their guests did not know was that Peter and Lily were already married. At sunrise, they professed their love for each other and became husband and wife. When the evening winded down and they found themselves back at home lying in bed, Peter slid his hair through her shimmering blond hair, kissed her on the forehead and whispered into his ear that she was his 'beautiful flower'. Married life hadn't changed either one of them. Time moved forward and the years went by but Peter and Lily always found time to laugh together, to hold hands as much as possible and to be devoted to each other no matter what.

They didn't have any children and believed that was how it was supposed to be just as the way they met.

"What is meant to be, will be," Lily used to always say. The words spoken from her lips couldn't have been truer.

Days turned into months, and months into years. Dark hair turned to almost none at all. Blonde hair turned white. Neither of which bothered them. Peter and Lily did almost everything together. It was hard to see one without the other by their side. They were the perfect match in every way. When the right pieces to a puzzle are found, they slide together without a hitch. One afternoon, Peter had returned home from the store to find Lily asleep on the couch. He placed the bags of groceries on the counter and crouched down beside her. He took her hand into his and gently spoke to her to let her know he was home. Her eyes slowly opened and she smiled. When she went to sit up, she felt a little dizzy and said her head hadn't stopped hurting all day even with the aid of some aspirin. Peter told her to lie back down and rest. When the evening came, Lily still complained of a headache. They followed their normal evening routine—dinner together, watching their favourite TV show and then climbing into bed. The following morning, the sun came beaming through their bedroom windows. Peter's hand lifted his face and slid down, letting fingers rub against his eyes before they blinked a few times to adjust to the light. He rolled over expecting to wrap his arms around his beautiful flower but Lily wasn't in bed.

*She must be already having her coffee and breakfast,* he thought.

Peter gave one more stretch of his arms and then rolled out of bed with his feet hitting the floor with a thud. He grabbed his robe and placed his arms down through the sleeves and then made a loose knot out of the belt around his waist. He made his way down the stairs and into the kitchen. The coffee pot wasn't on and there wasn't the smell of anything being cooked. Peter called out for her.

"Lily?" No response. His voice grew a little louder with a small bit of panic attached. "Lily!?" Once again he was greeted with silence. He quickly went to one of the windows looking out over the garage. The car was still here. Peter could feel his heart pounding in his chest as he ran from the kitchen and back up the steps. As he reached the top step, he noticed that the bathroom door was ajar and he could see her feet as they rested on the floor. Peter walked over and pushed the door open. Lily was sitting on the toilet with the cover down. Her head was in her hands and she was sobbing. Peter slowly walked over to her and knelt down in front of her, placing his hand onto hers. His voice was soft as his other hand softly went down through her grey hair.

"Lily. What's wrong honey? Are you okay?"

Lily did not utter a word. Her sobs came even harder now. It broke Peter's heart to see the love of his life like this. He let her cry. He held her close and just let her tears soak into his shoulder. After a few minutes, Lily broke the embrace and looked into Peter's eyes. Her cheeks were stained with wet streaks and her voice was a little raspy from all the crying.

"When I woke up this morning, I came to the bathroom. Then… ummm… then I… I couldn't remember where I was."

"You couldn't remember where you were?" Peter reiterated.

Lily's head nodded yes. Immediately Peter wrapped her in a long embrace.

"C'mon, my flower. Maybe you had a bad dream that disoriented you and the dizziness is because you're hungry. Let's go downstairs and I'll make you some breakfast."

With Peter's assistance, Lily stood back to her feet. She said she felt better and they headed downstairs to the kitchen. Peter cooked some bacon and eggs and made a fresh pot of coffee. Sitting at the table, Lily said she felt better now that she ate. They talked about what their day was looking like before a look of concern adorned Peter's face.

"I think you should go see the doctor just to get a check-up."

"It's just headaches, Peter," said Lily.

"I know, baby. They have medicine that's strong for those types of headaches, right?"

"What are they called? Mi... uhhh... Mi... damn... what's the word?"

"Migraines."

"Yes! That's what I was thinking of."

Lily smiled and laughed at how Peter could never remember simple things but he could tell you every state capital even if you didn't ask.

"Alright, my love," said Lily. "I'll give the doctor a call and make an appointment."

Peter smiled at her and mouthed the words, "Thank you," before he leant in and gave her a peck to the cheek. Once breakfast was finished, Lily called the doctor and her appointment was set for the next day.

Lily was all set and ready to head to the doctors to hopefully get some stronger medication to get rid of the headaches. She walked into the living room where Peter was watching TV and leant over to give him a kiss goodbye. When she stood back up, she stumbled backwards, her back hitting the wall. Peter sprang from the couch and quickly grabbed her arm to help steady her. She sucked in a deep breath and eventually straightened herself up to a proper stand. She didn't have to mention she felt dizzy, weak or her legs were a little numb. The man who loved her ever since they met knew her better than he knew himself. Peter already has his coat on and the keys in his hand. He slipped his hand into hers. Their palms fit together perfectly and the way their fingers intertwined made it obvious they were put together because they were meant for each other. They left the house and Peter helped Lily into the car and they drove to go and see the doctor. Peter's mind struggled with the fact what was happening with his Lily was more than just headaches. Lily didn't have to struggle with those same thoughts at all. She knew there was more going on with her and it scared her to death, though for the entire car ride they smiled at each other and had their usual normal conversations.

*A doctor's office always smells funny,* Peter thought.

He could never put his finger on the smell but even during the war, the medical tents seemed to smell the same. Maybe it's all the medicine they use. He looked around at all the paintings that adorned the wall. Then he looked at Lily. She was sitting in the chair, legs crossed, reading one of the magazines the office supplied to its patients. Was he the only one who couldn't focus enough to read? Lily looked so calm, he thought. The nurse opened the door and called out Lily's name. She stood and took a breath, hoping that one of her dizzy spells wouldn't happen. Peter stood up as well and took her hand into his. She could feel his strength and that provided her with such comfort. They walked into the examination room together and waited to see the doctor. Upon the conclusion of the appointment, the doctor had ordered Lily to go get a blood test and when she did, he would then call her with the results in a few days.

The telephone rang and in her usual pleasant voice, Lily answered with a "Hello?" On the other end of the line was the doctor. Once he shared the blood test results with her, he then told her that an MRI has been scheduled for the next day. Lily didn't say much as she stood there processing the news. How was she going to break the news to Peter? Further testing wasn't something she expected to hear. Lily was ripped from her thoughts when the telephone began to make that off the hook warning sound. She hung up the phone and could feel streaks of wetness falling down her cheeks. She wiped them away and went to find Peter. They have always been open and honest with each other. She'd tell him the news right away. He was outside in the garden when she found him. She came up behind him and slid her arms around his waist and rested her head against his back. He smiled for a moment and then turned around. Lily didn't have to say a word. He knew her better than he knew himself. Her blue eyes told the story. Something was wrong. He wrapped his arms around her and pulled her into him. Muffled against his chest, she shared with him the news. "It's just an MRI. They just want to make sure everything is okay, which I'm sure it is," Peter told himself.

They were sitting on the couch together watching one of their favourite black and white movies when the telephone rang. Lily patted Peter's leg as she stood up to go answer it. She stood there with the phone to her ear in complete silence. Eventually, she mustered up a small 'thank you' and hung up the phone. Instantly, she placed her hands over her eyes and began to sob uncontrollably. Peter could hear her and he jumped off the couch and rushed to where she stood crying.

"Lily. What is it?"

"The results... I... they said..."

The tears fell freely from her eyes.

"There's a tumour in my brain."

Peter stood there shocked and could think of nothing to say except to walk over to her and wrap his arms around her. Lily turned to face him and buried her face into his chest.

"I'm scared, Peter."

"I know, baby. I know. Let's see what the doctor says. There's treatments and surgery that can fix you."

Peter placed both hands on Lily's cheeks, his palms soaking with her tears. He looked into her eyes.

"We will figure this all out together, my beautiful flower. You're not going to deal with this alone. I'll be right there with you every step of the way no matter what."

Lily nodded her head and then buried herself back into Peter's chest. They had always been there for each other even when they were living apart. Nothing would change now. She will need him even more now than ever. He knew this and would give her all the strength he can.

"Surgery is the first step we'd take in dealing with the type of brain tumour you have. This will allow us to take a biopsy, remove as much of the tumour as we can and also provide relief for you. I understand your headaches have been very severe. Then we will proceed with radiation and chemotherapy with the hope we can slow down the residual tumours the surgery could not remove."

Everything the doctor was saying sounded like a bunch of blurry words to Lily. She heard all she needed to the other day when the phone call happened. She was diagnosed with a Glioblastoma brain tumour, which is the most common primary brain tumour. Lily immediately began to read up on that specific kind of tumour and quickly discovered that Glioblastoma is the most common primary brain cancer. They are Grade IV tumours. She was scared to death but was not going to just give up. The squeeze Peter's hand gave her snapped her from her thoughts and back to reality. The doctor's voice seemingly came back into focus. She nodded her head before looking him in the eyes.

"And if the treatments don't work and there can be no surgery, how much time do I have, doctor?"

"Well… according to studies and data, 12 to 18 months."

The doctor paused. Lily's head lifted with a stubborn pride as she held back the tears that were threatening to cascade down her cheeks. Peter was not as stoic. Wetness adorned his cheeks as he squeezed his flower's hand. The doctor drew in a breath and then let it out slowly. Delivering news such as this was never easy. It was the part of his job that he despised the most.

"There have been new studies that have shown there has been success in beating this. We will do all we can to see that you're one of the success stories."

Peter and Lily both thanked the doctor as he left the examination room. They sat in silence with their hands intertwined and squeezed together like two snakes suffocating prey. Their eyes met. They both had served in the war. They'd both fought in life.

They'd fought for each other. This fight was different. It would be difficult. It would be trying. They would be tested, but Peter and Lily were ready. Together they could be anything. She was the strongest person he'd ever met. She was not in this alone. Lily knew whether it was 12 months or 12 years, she had him. Peter was all the strength she'd need to beat this.

The sun rose and its rays tried to sneak their way past the drawn blinds. The room was kept dark to help with the headaches. Surgery was scheduled for tomorrow. Lily and Peter lay in bed, her back nestled into his chest. He lay behind her with his hand sliding down through her now-grey locks. Her hair was once a shimmering blonde but time carries on and stops for no one. The hair colour never mattered to Peter. She was beautiful to him no matter what. There was silence between them and he could hear the pounding of Lily's heart. This caused him to hold her tighter.

"I'm scared," she whispered.

"I know. Me too," was all Peter said in reply and they lay there without words from the day until the evening when they both fell asleep again. When they would awake tomorrow, Lily would be headed for one of the most important battles of her life—of their lives.

Lily's eyes slowly opened, then closed and then opened again as they started to focus. There was a faint beeping sound that seemed like it was in the distance. She felt Peter's hand in hers and could see the smile on his face.

*I'm either in heaven or I've made it through the surgery,* she thought to herself.

The doctor's voice invaded her thoughts and she was told the surgery was as successful as they could've hoped for. Everything that had been previously discussed was coming to fruition. Soon enough, Lily would begin her chemotherapy. Once she was up and out of the bed, she began her treatments. In the beginning, Lily felt weak and tired but she relied on Peter's strength to help push her through. When her once-blonde, now-silvery hair all fell out, he made sure she knew she was still his beautiful flower. One day after a treatment, Lily was laying on the couch relaxing and watching TV. Peter knelt down next to her and took her hand into his. He leant forward and placed a kiss on her forehead. He asked how she was feeling and Lily said despite the treatments, she was actually feeling better than she thought.

Peter smiled, "We should take a little trip."

"A trip? Where to?" Lily asked.

"I have a place in mind. It's not too far away and we'll be back in time for your next treatment. It's nice and quiet. Trust me."

Peter gave a huge Cheshire-like grin which made Lily laugh and smile. She nodded her head yes, and after dinner, they would pack their bags for the car ride. She was excited and this was the distraction they both needed. The car ride to their destination was filled with wonderful scenery. The leaves on the trees were beginning to turn red, yellow and orange. When Peter drove the car, what seemed like off the road, a dirt path took them down a dark pathway because all the trees were preventing sunlight from peeking through. As they drove a little bit further, a small cabin appeared in the distance. Lily turned to Peter with excitement plastered all over her face. Once the car was parked, Peter hopped out of the car and walked to the other side and opened Lily's door. She was still weakened from her treatments, so he assisted her. Once out of the car, Lily couldn't contain her excitement. The little cabin was perfect. There were two rocking chairs on the porch and when she went inside, she immediately explored the kitchen and bedroom. Peter walked in behind her and brought the suitcases to the bedroom. That's when he heard Lily's shriek of excitement. Peter casually walked from the bedroom to the living room and stood there with a smile on his face. Lily was still speechless as she stared at the two large bookshelves that ran from floor to ceiling and were filled with so much to read.

"Do you love it?" asked Peter. Lily walked over to him, wrapped her arms around his neck and gave him a long kiss. When their lips separated, Peter replied with: "I'll take that as a yes."

The next morning, Peter awoke and rolled over only to find the other side of the bed empty. He could still see the imprint from where she lay and the scent of her invaded his senses. The smell of his Lily had always intoxicated his senses and he'd have it no other way. Peter stretched and pulled the covers off then slid out of the bed. Before he walked into the kitchen to see if Lily was there sipping her coffee already, he noticed something. Resting on the dresser was the grey wig Lily had been wearing.

Once the treatments began, she lost her hair and preferred to wear a wig because she was so self-conscious about her look. Peter recalled how vibrantly blonde her hair was when they first met and how it gradually turned grey over the years. On his way to the door, his fingers lightly glided over the wig before he made his way into the kitchen. He came around the corner only to find no one sitting in the chair at the table. He wondered where Lily went. He made his way through the living room, and as he did, he looked out of the window and there she was. Lily was standing on the porch. Her head held high, letting the sun warm her face and her head. This was the first time Peter saw her sans hair and she looked beautiful. Lily raised her arms, and from Peter's view, it looked like she was embracing the sun in a hug. The longer he watched her, Peter could not help but to wipe a tear from his eyes. Lily looked like an angel spreading her wings. The sun was brighter now and its rays made her silhouette look stunning. Finally, Peter opened the door and stepped outside. He walked up behind Lily and slid his hands around her waist. She leant back against him. Peter said nothing and just placed a kiss on her head. Together they stood watching the sun rise into the sky higher and higher. They forgot about everything for a little while and just soaked in their surroundings and the quiet peacefulness it offered them.

Their little getaway was going by fast. Peter and Lily soaked in and enjoyed every moment they were there. They would take morning walks and marvel at how the foliage was changing into vibrant colours. After a well-cooked dinner, they would sit and read together or cuddle up on the couch and watch a movie. These were all the perfect distractions needed but soon it would be time to go home and Lily would resume her treatments. On their last night of the trip, Lily and Peter sat outside by a small fire they had made and they reminisced about the day they met. They laughed and smiled as they recalled every last detail. They both admitted to each other that those memories felt just like they were made yesterday. The next morning, they both took in one more sunrise before the car was packed and they headed back home and back to the reality there was no more escape from.

"I'm very sorry to say that with the radiation and chemotherapy that the tumour hasn't really shrunk. Now we can continue with the same course of action in hopes for it to still shrink down." The white light in the examination room seemed to be shining brighter than normal and Lily felt the need to keep squinting her eyes. As she adjusted her eyesight, Peter came into focus followed by the voice of the doctor. It was as if Lily had zoned out and already floated into the white light people claim they see before they die. The words from the doctor took a moment to settle and register in her brain.

Finally, she blurted out, "No!" This one word carried so much meaning; it stunned the doctor and he stopped speaking. Peter came closer to the examination table to place his hand in hers. Lily continued, "I don't want anymore. If it's not working, I don't want anymore. I'm tired all the time. I've lost my hair. The vomiting. The body aches. All for what? If it's not working, then I don't want to continually do this to myself."

The doctor nodded his head. "Very well. I'll give you both a minute. When you're done, the nurse will have some paperwork for you to sign. Again, I'm very sorry." Then the doctor left the room, closing the door behind him.

"If you stop now, then God knows how much time you have left," said Peter.

"I'm willing to leave it to God's hands. The treatments aren't working, Peter. I don't want to live the rest of whatever life I have left letting some medicine poison me more and more and all I get from it is feeling horrible. I'll get some strength back. We can travel again. Maybe spend more time at the cabin. The scenery was so beautiful." Lily offered Peter a smile. Her smile always melted him. "If that is your wish, then I support you. Always." Peter gave her hand a squeeze and they walked out of the examination room.

They will live life to its fullest, the best they could for as long as they could.

As the following weeks went on, Lily started to feel more like herself despite the tumour on her brain. Since she decided to stop the treatments, she felt a little more like herself each day. The vomiting ceased despite some headaches and a little disorientation here and there. She was gaining her strength back, which made her want to do more and more with Peter. Even some of her hair started to slowly grow back. She was still self-conscious about that though and continued to wear her wig. She and Peter began to plan out what they were going to do with whatever time would be afforded to them. Neither one of them discussed what the future would hold nor what most likely will happen. Peter and Lily took this time to enjoy each other even more than ever. They'd come a long way since the day they met and life had thrown its fair share of curves their way but they always believed that together they'd be able to take anything on. Right now was the ultimate proof of that. What they could control, they would, and the rest would be left in the hands of God.

Peter and Lily began to enjoy experiences such as watching the sunrise while they sat in their backyard. That's something they never did before. They would take a nightly walk around the neighbourhood just to soak in the fresh early evening air. Sometimes they would converse with each other the entire walk, and other times they simply remained silent and just relished each other's company. There were still times Lily would wake in the middle of the night confused or have a crippling headache during the day that would leave her lying on the couch in the darkened room. Yet no episode or pounding in her head could stop them. There were trips to the mountains where they could enjoy looking at the world in a way they never thought they'd be able to see. Lily and Peter took themselves on experiences that they probably would've never thought they'd do, such as learning how to ballroom dance and play craps at the casino. They never seemed to win anything but enjoyed it nonetheless. Time was flying by, it seemed, but neither one of them discussed that or worried. It didn't have to be said that Lily's time wasn't going to be as long as they would like it to be. Sitting at dinner and discussing dying was not something they were interested in. Instead, Peter and Lily focused on all the memories they were making. On their many excursions, Peter would take lots of photos and then make sure they were put into an album. Every moment they shared, he wanted to be frozen in time.

One particular week, Lily was having a really hard time. Peter would find her disorientated in the middle of the night or in the early morning. She would wander through the house and think the bathroom was the kitchen and the living room was the garage. Each time he found her, Peter would talk softly to her and be able to guide her back to bed. During the day, her headaches were so bad that she was constantly vomiting and could barely open her eyes. She would complain about the aches in her body and how intense they were. No matter what, Peter remained by her side and brought her what she needed and saw to her care. Even when Lily would lash out because of the unbearable headaches, Peter would absorb it and sit with her. He knew that wasn't really Lily talking.

*She's been through so much,* he thought.

Never once did he become angry with her. He was going to always be by her side like he promised her all those years ago.

Lily started to feel a little better once again. She had made it through some tough episodes. Peter woke one morning and rolled over only to find the other side of the bed empty. He got out of bed hoping that Lily hadn't had a spell that disoriented her again. Once his feet touched the floor, he heard it. It was Lily's voice calling to him. Peter left the bedroom and descended down the stairs. The smell of eggs, bacon and coffee filled the air. He entered the kitchen and Lily gave him a smile as she placed food on a plate.

"Good morning, sleepy head," said Lily.

With a smile on his face as he sat down at the table, Peter said, "Well, good morning to you too. Food smells delicious. Are you sure you should be—"

"Cooking? Standing up? I feel good, Peter. The sun is shining. The birds are chirping. Can't have a better morning for a good breakfast."

She gave him a wink and then sat down at the table as well. The conversation between them was still engaging all these years later. They never lacked when it came to speaking to each other. There was always something to say.

"Peter?" Lily asked.

"Yes?" he answered in between chewing and swallowing.

"Remember that cabin? I'd love to go back. It was so pretty up there and I found so much peace."

Peter didn't have to even give it any thought. He told her he would call and reserve the cabin for the nearest date, which turned out to be the upcoming weekend. Lily couldn't contain her excitement. She finished eating and kissed Peter on the cheek and then went to already start packing. Peter remained at the table and a few little tears rolled down his cheeks. This may be the happiest he'd seen her in a long time and he wanted to hold onto this image of her forever.

They found themselves back at the little cabin once more. The second time around seemed even more magical than the first time. Peter and Lily felt like they were having a different experience than they had before. The leaves on the trees seemed brighter. The air was fresher. The way the sunlight lit up the rooms every morning even seemed to take on a new meaning. This time around, Peter was sure to bring his camera to capture moments in time. Just as before, he awoke to find Lily outside on the porch with the sun rising. With camera in hand, he began to snap picture after picture. With her arms spread out wide, it looked like she was hugging the sun. The sun created what looked like wings around her. It may have not really been her hair but the wind was blowing her white tresses in the wind. Peter stood in awe once more. She was so beautiful. How can someone this lovely on the inside and outside only have a few months to live? She should be able to finish out her life. No one ever gets to choose their terms when it's their time to meet their maker but Lily deserved a longer life. If Peter could've switched places with her, he would have without a thought. After letting the sun soak into her skin, making her feel more alive than she had in months, Lily turned to see Peter and his camera. She walked over to him and together they looked at the photos.

"You look like an angel," Peter said. Lily took the camera from his hands.

"Your turn," she said.

"But I take awful pictures."

"Nonsense. Now get over there and let me take a few of you."

Peter moved from Lily and with the railing of the porch to his back, he turned to face her and he plastered a smile to his face and she took some photos. Once she was finished and lowered the camera, Lily told him she was going to go back inside. Peter said he'd be there in a minute and he turned around to let the sun warm his face. He tilted his head back and just breathed in the fresh air. Unbeknownst to him, Lily was snapping some more pictures. When Peter turned to enter the cabin, he found her lying on the couch relaxing. He joined her and they settled in to watch a movie. It was time once again to say goodbye to the cabin that Lily and Peter had come to love so much. Peter was packing the car, and once finished, he climbed in and started it. Lily emerged from the inside and slowly walked down the steps. She turned to soak in the image of the cabin one more time. This was most likely the last time she was going to see this place. Peter knew exactly what she was doing. Lily came to the car. They said nothing and drove off. The cabin became smaller and smaller the further they drove away. Lily turned around and looked one last time at the tiny speck that was the cabin. She really did love it here.

They had been home for a few weeks now since their trip to the cabin. Peter had the pictures developed and couldn't wait to add them to the memory album. Lily joined him and they laughed at the ones they took with silly faces and they gave each other's hand a squeeze at the more romantic pictures. The 'angel photo'—as Peter called it—was not put into the album but put into a frame instead and would find a place on Peter's nightstand. Lily had removed the picture she took of Peter and had it framed and she would find the right time to surprise him with it. He had no idea she photographed with the sunrise serving as a backdrop the same way he did her. One afternoon, Peter was sitting on the couch when Lily entered the room and placed a wrapped box onto his lap.

"What's this?" he asked.

"Open it and find out," said Lily with a hint of excitement in her voice. Peter ripped off the wrapping paper and opened the box. He lifted out the frame and was speechless at the contents within. It was the picture Lily took of him.

Before he could speak, she said, "That's how I see you. As an angel ascending from heaven. My angel. There's no way I could get through this without you by my side." Peter felt the tears stinging his eyes. He said nothing. His lips meeting hers was more than any words he could've articulated. Every night before Peter closed his eyes for sleep, he'd look to his nightstand and there was the picture of Lily, and right next to it was the one of him.

He'd smile before closing his eyes and let dreams take him away.

Peter and Lily had made some unforgettable memories but those were to soon be overshadowed by the truth they both had been trying to pretend wasn't there. Lily's brain tumour did not shrink with the treatments. There was going to be no surgery. Neither one of them discussed what could happen, but life doesn't stop or slow down for anyone. It had been a few weeks since they'd gone anywhere and that was because Lily's health is starting its downward spiral. Peter was used to waking up to her voice calling out to him, and on this particular morning, it wasn't there. He got out of bed and found Lily standing in the living room seemingly staring out of the window. When he asked her what was wrong, she replied that she was about to start breakfast. Lily was becoming more disorientated. Her headaches were back and even more viscous than before. She spent countless times in the bathroom getting sick. Reality of the situation was kicking in. Peter did the best he could to help her. If she hit a state of confusion, he made sure he redirected her to whatever task she was going to do. He brought her aspirin and cold packs for her when the headaches kicked in. He held her hair back when she needed to get sick. Peter refused to leave Lily's side through all of this. She would apologise profusely to him and he always responded with the kindest words and told her that no matter what, she wasn't going to be alone through this. Peter also noticed that Lily's appetite seemed to be decreasing. Sometimes she would eat half of what was on her plate and other times she didn't want anything. He could see the change in her body as the weight seemed to begin to melt off. She would claim she was always thirsty, but at times, she couldn't even swallow water, and when she did, she wasn't able to keep it down. So as she would rest, Peter brought her a cup of ice cubes to be able to suck on, and when they melted in her mouth, the cold water produced felt so good. Lily still attended visits with the doctor and when she remembered, she would explain what she was experiencing and when she couldn't, Peter would do so for her. As the doctor had stated before, there wasn't much that could be done for Lily except to try and make her as comfortable as possible, which Lily would refuse, stating that she did not want to be bedridden until the end. She was determined to try and do her normal everyday activities regardless of the fact her body was betraying her. Each time Peter heard the news from the doctor, it broke his heart, but at the same time, he was inspired by Lily's fight and unwillingness to give up. He understood what would happen the day she refused anymore treatments because they weren't working. He got time with her while she still felt good and strong. As much as he didn't want what was happening to come, it was here and he was going to have to face that. Sooner than later, he would be without his beautiful flower and that terrified him to think how he'd be able to go on without her by his side every day. The doctor did mention that the symptoms will only get worse and the best course of action would be to eventually get Lily into a hospital where they can try and make her as comfortable as possible. Lily simply looked at the doctor, then to Peter, then back to the doctor and stated matter-of-factly, "When it's time for me to meet my maker, I will not die in some hospital room. I will die at home where I belong."

No one was going to be able to argue with her or change her mind. Lily knew her time was running out and wanted to cross over to the other side on her terms. She couldn't control what her body was doing to her but she most certainly could control where she would draw her final breath.

Each day that passed, Peter did his best to hold his emotions inside and keep a brave face. Every day he looked at Lily, he could see her becoming thinner and it pained his heart to see the pain she was in. But she never complained. He admired her more and more. Even though she started to look less and less like the woman he first met all those years ago, Peter's love never wavered. He told Lily that as cliché as it sounded, he promised her on their wedding day: "… and in sickness and in health." When Lily was struggling and having a day when she couldn't remember very much, Peter brought out a greenish photo album with the words: *"Our Memories"* written on it. He sat down next to Lily, and when he opened the album, he began to flip through the pictures of their wedding day and pictures of their travels including the cabin they both grew to really love visiting. He would smile and laugh as he remembered something funny right before one of the photos was taken. At times, Lily would do the same and recall some memories and other times she had almost no idea what he was talking about then would say how her head was hurting and she needed to lie down. His flower was wilting. Peter knew what the eventual outcome would be but there was no way he was prepared to not have his Lily by his side.

It was a Monday and that familiar sunrise made its presence known by shining light and warmth through the bedroom window. Slowly, Peter's eyes opened. The birds serenaded each other outside his window but something was missing. That lovely voice of his flower—his Lily—was not calling to him. Peter rolled to his side and the sunrise was now an eclipse. His Lily, his light, had died in her sleep. The tears freely spilled from Peter's eyes and he wrapped his arms around her. He held her close, and just as he always did, his fingers stroked the white cloud of hair upon her head which had started to grow back. His warm lips kissed her cold ones and then they kissed her wrinkly forehead for the last time. Now, Lily was gone. She sat up in the heavens and watched over her beloved Peter. Life for Peter would be forever changed. He was alone and had to adjust to being so but the routine they started years ago never changed. Every sunrise, Peter woke up to the same familiar light shining through the window. He would roll over and now his arms held nothing but air. He would pause a moment and listen for her voice to call to him to come downstairs because breakfast was ready. A picture of Lily stood on the nightstand next to the bed and next to her picture was the one she had taken of him. And in between their photos sat the greenish wedding album filled with their memories. Her crystal blue eyes showing so much life with a captivating smile in the picture stared Peter in the face. He leant over and pressed his lips to the glass. When he pulled away, he swore he could taste the sweetness of her lips and feel the tenderness of her touch. Now as the sun rose, then set and then rose again, Peter repeated everything he did with Lily from the moment his eyes adjusted to the light to when the darkness put him to sleep. As he lay in bed, Peter whispered to the heavens to let his beautiful flower know that his love for her never died. Sleep then took Peter, and in comfort he rested. When the sunrise appeared and shone its yellow light through the window to illuminate the bedroom, and when the birds chirped their songs, Peter's eyes did not open, but he was happy. The next time Peter saw Lily, she was young, happy and pain-free. Peter once again held Lily tightly in his loving arms. A chance meeting between two people turned into a love story for the ages. Peter and Lily lived side by side and walked through life smiling and holding hands even when at times they were given obstacles to overcome. As the sun continued to rise and set, it did over two grey stones which stood firmly in the grass of the graveyard they belonged to. Peter and Lily would remain side by side in death as they did in life.

www.ingramcontent.com/pod-product-compliance
Lightning Source LLC
Chambersburg PA
CBHW071256130726
47998CB00003B/1221